Words to Know Before You Read

electricity

Grandpa

paint

recycle

reduce

remember

reuse

school

waste

www.rourkepublishing.com

Edited by Luana K. Mitten
Illustrated by Anita DuFalla
Art Direction and Page Layout by Renee Brady

Library of Congress Cataloging-in-Publication Data

Robertson, J. Jean
 Grandpa Comes to First Grade / J. Jean Robertson.
   p. cm. -- (Little Birdie Books)
 ISBN 978-1-61741-800-6 (hard cover) (alk. paper)
 ISBN 978-1-61236-004-1 (soft cover)
 Library of Congress Control Number: 2011924652

Rourke Publishing
Printed in China, Voion Industry
   Guangdong Province
042011
042011LP

www.rourkepublishing.com - rourke@rourkepublishing.com
Post Office Box 643328 Vero Beach, Florida 32964

GRANDPA COMES
to First Grade

By J. Jean Robertson
Illustrated by Anita DuFalla

"Grandpa, I'm so glad you can visit my school. You know, my school is green."

"No, I didn't know."

"We learn the three R's of living green."

I ♥ 🌍 Reduce

Reuse

Recycle

"We don't waste paper."

"We don't waste water."

"We don't get something new if we can use something we already have."

18

"We like LIVING GREEN. You can do it too!"

21

After Reading Activities

You and the Story...

What did Jada mean when she said her school was *green*?

Name three things that Jada and her classmates taught Grandpa about being green.

Is your school a green school? If not, what could you do to make your school green?

Words You Know Now...

Choose three of the words below. On a piece of paper write a new sentence for each of the three words you chose.

electricity	remember
Grandpa	reuse
paint	school
recycle	waste
reduce	

You Could...Start Your Own Recycling Program

- Make a list of the things you can recycle.

- Decide where you are going to start your recycling program (home or school).

- Make signs or posters to promote recycling.

- Research where you can take materials to be recycled.

- Make recycling boxes to collect materials to be recycled.

About the Author

J. Jean Robertson, also known as Bushka to her grandchildren and many other kids, lives in San Antonio, Florida with her husband. She is retired after many years of teaching. One way Bushka lives green is by saving old newspapers and magazines for her grandson. He takes them to his school to be recycled.

About the Illustrator

Acclaimed for its versatility in style, Anita DuFalla's work has appeared in many educational books, newspaper articles, and business advertisements and on numerous posters, book and magazine covers, and even giftwraps. Anita's passion for pattern is evident in both her artwork and her collection of 400 patterned tights. She lives in the Friendship neighborhood of Pittsburgh, Pennsylvania with her son, Lucas.